TEN SMALL TALES

TEN
SMALL
TALES

TOLD BY
Celia Barker Lottridge

PICTURES BY
Joanne Fitzgerald

A GROUNDWOOD BOOK

Douglas & McIntyre
Toronto/Vancouver

For my mother, Louise Shedd Barker,
who tells stories for all ages—CBL

For Lynne—JF

Text copyright © 1993 by Celia Barker Lottridge
Illustrations copyright © 1993 by Joanne Fitzgerald
Second printing 1999

The publisher gratefully acknowledges the assistance of the Canada Council for the Arts, the Ontario Arts Council and the Government of Canada through the Book Publishing Industry Development Program for our publishing activities.

Groundwood Books / Douglas & McIntyre
585 Bloor Street West
Toronto, Ontario M6G 1K5

Distributed in the USA by Publishers Group West
1700 Fourth Street
Berkeley, CA 94710

Canadian Cataloguing in Publication Data

Lottridge, Celia B. (Celia Barker)
Ten small tales
ISBN 0-88899-156-8
1. Tales. I. Fitzgerald, Joanne, 1956-
II. Title.
PS8573.O88T46 1993   j398.2   C93-093859-3
PZ8.1.L78Te 1993

The author would like to acknowledge the support of the Regina Public Library
Writer-in-Residence Program.

The illustrations are done in watercolour, ink and Conté crayon.
Printed and bound in China by Everbest Printing Co. Ltd.

CONTENTS

Four Legs, Four Arms, One Head

A MAN and his small son were walking through the jungle one afternoon. They were hurrying to get home, but darkness came while they still had far to go.

The man looked around and said, "There is a soft patch of grass here beside the river. We'll lie down and rest until the moon comes up and gives us light."

The little boy looked around at the shadowy jungle and said, "All right, but I want to sleep in the middle."

"But there are only two of us," said his father. "You can't sleep in the middle. Lie close beside me on this side."

"No! No! No!" said the little boy. "I want to sleep in the middle."

"Shhhh," said his father. "You can't sleep in the middle. Lie close beside me on the other side."

"No! No! No!" said the little boy. "I want to sleep in the middle."

"Try this," said his father. "I'll lie on my back and you lie on my middle, with your head on my belly and your legs between my legs and your arms under my arms. There. Is that better?"

"Yes," said the little boy. He could feel his father breathing, his belly going in and out, in and out. Pretty soon the boy fell asleep.

As the man and the little boy lay sleeping, a tiger came slinking along the riverbank. He was hoping to find something good to eat, and when he saw a lumpy shape lying in the shadows beside the river, he crept closer to see what it was.

He looked hard. Something was not right. He blinked.

He saw four legs. He saw four arms. But he saw only one head, because the little boy's head was right in the middle, hidden in the shadows.

The tiger was so surprised that he ran down to the river and called, "Friend Crocodile, listen to me. There is a strange creature asleep on the riverbank. It has four legs and four arms and only one head! How can this be?"

The crocodile stuck his long nose out of the water and laughed. "You must have counted wrong," he said. "There is no animal with four legs, four arms, and one head. Go and count again."

So the tiger went back. Being a tiger he counted by sniffing. He sniffed at the legs of the strange creature. One, two, three, four. He sniffed at the arms. One, two on one side, three, four on the other side. He sniffed at the head he could see and that was the father's head. Just one head!

But he sniffed so close that his whiskers tickled the father's nose. All of a sudden the father sneezed a huge sneeze. *"AaahteChooo!"* When he sneezed, his belly jumped, and the little boy sat up and said, *"Yow!"*

The tiger was so surprised that he jumped backward into the river.

The father stood up very quickly, picked up the little boy, and said, "The moon is up and it is giving us dreams. Let's go home now." And they did.

By the time the tiger got out of the river they were gone. So the tiger went home, too, and told his own little tigers about the strange creature that had four legs, four arms, and one head, and said, *"AaahteChooo! Yow!"*

The Fox and
the Walking Stick

A FOX was going along a road one day when she saw a walking stick lying in a ditch.

"Now that might come in handy," she said to herself. So she stuck it in her sack and away she went down the road.

Toward evening she came to a little house. She knocked on the door. *Stook-stook! Stook-stook!*

A woman opened the door.

"May I come in and sleep by your stove?" asked the fox.

"Oh, no," said the woman. "We hardly have room for ourselves."

"I'll curl up in the corner with my tail over my nose and my walking stick under the bench," said the fox. "You won't know I'm there."

So they let the fox into the house, and she put her walking stick under the bench and curled up with her tail over her nose. But very early in the morning she woke up and put her walking stick into the stove and burned it up.

When the people woke up the fox said, "My walking stick is gone! My walking stick is gone! You must give me a chicken instead."

She made such a fuss that the people gave her a chicken, and the fox put it in her sack and set off down the road.

Toward evening she came to a little house. She knocked on the door. *Stook-stook! Stook-stook!*

A man came to the door.

"May I come in and sleep by your stove?" asked the fox.

"Oh, no," said the man. "We hardly have room for ourselves."

"I'll curl up in the corner with my tail over my nose and my chicken under the bench," said the fox. "You won't know I'm there."

So they let her in, and she curled up in the corner and put the chicken under the bench. But very early in the morning she woke up and ate the chicken, every bit.

When the people woke up the fox said, "My chicken is gone! My chicken is gone! You must give me a goose instead."

She made such a fuss that the people gave her a goose, and the fox put it in her sack and set off down the road.

Toward evening she came to the house of a shepherd. She knocked on the door. *Stook-stook! Stook-stook!*

The shepherd came to the door.

"May I come in and sleep by your stove?" asked the fox.

"Oh, no," said the shepherd. "We hardly have room for ourselves."

But his children said, "Look how pretty the fox is. Let it in. Let it in." So the shepherd let the fox in. She curled up in the corner with her tail over her nose and put the goose under the bench.

In the morning she woke up very early and ate up the goose, all but one feather. When the people woke up she cried out, "My goose is gone! My goose is gone! You must give me a lamb instead."

[14]

She made such a fuss that the shepherd took her sack out to his lamb pen. But he really did not want to give one of his lambs to the fox, and besides that, he had noticed one goose feather on the end of her nose. So instead of a lamb he put his good little watchdog in the sack.

The fox picked up the sack and said to herself, "That's a nice fat lamb," and down the road she went. After a while she thought she would stop and take a peek at the lamb, but as soon as she opened the sack out jumped the dog!

The fox began to run and the dog ran after her. They ran and ran. Just when the fox thought she could run no farther, she saw a hole under a rock. It was just big enough for her and in she went. She could hear the dog sniffing outside, but she knew he couldn't squeeze in.

The fox said, "Little feet, little feet, how did you help me get away from the dog?"

Her feet answered, "We ran as fast as we could."

"Thank you," said the fox. "Little eyes, little eyes, what did you do?"

Her eyes answered, "We watched for every stick and stone so that you could run fast."

"Thank you," said the fox. "Little nose, little nose, what did you do?"

Her nose answered, "I sniffed out the best trail for you to follow."

"Thank you," said the fox. "Little tail, little tail, what did you do?"

"Oh," said the tail, "I didn't do anything."

"Then you can't stay in here with us," said the fox. And she stuck her tail out of the hole. The dog jumped on it and bit it right off.

So if you see a fox running around without a tail, you'll know which fox that is.

The Great Big Enormous Rock

ONCE there were four animals who lived on an island.
One was a very slow animal. A turtle!
One was a long, thin, slithering animal. A snake!
One was a small animal who hopped everywhere. A rabbit!

And one was a very large animal with flapping ears. An elephant!

Right in the middle of the island there was a tall mountain. On top of the tall mountain was a great big enormous rock. It was so big that it covered the top of the mountain.

The four animals looked at the rock every day. They said, "If that rock wasn't there we could climb the mountain and have a picnic." But every day the enormous rock was still there.

One day the turtle said, "I will climb the mountain and push the rock off the top." So up the mountain he went, *creepy, creepy, creepy*. When he got to the top he put the edge of his shell under the rock and he pushed and he pushed and he pushed. But the great big enormous rock did not budge.

Then the snake said, "I'll try, too." So up the mountain she went, *slither, slither, slither*. She coiled herself up like a spring and she pushed her tail against the rock. She pushed

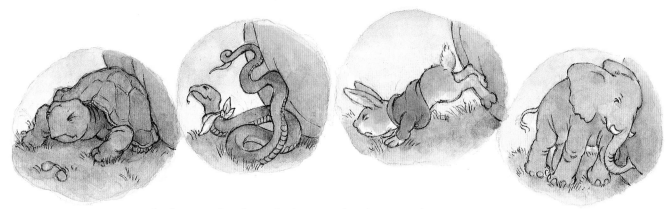

and she pushed and she pushed. But the great big enormous rock did not budge.

The rabbit said, "Now it's my turn." Up the mountain he went, *boing, boing, boing*. He put his strong back feet against the rock and he pushed and he pushed and he pushed. But the great big enormous rock did not budge.

The elephant laughed. "I'm the one to move the rock," she said. Up the mountain she went, *tromp, tromp, tromp*. She put her shoulder against the rock and she pushed and she pushed and she pushed. But the great big enormous rock did not budge.

The four animals looked at each other. "We will try it all together," they said. So the turtle pushed with his shell, the snake pushed with her tail, the rabbit pushed with his back feet, and the elephant pushed with her shoulder.

They pushed and they pushed and they pushed. They pushed again. And the great big enormous rock went *bumpity, bumpity, bumpity, bumpity,* CRASH! and it broke into a million pieces at the bottom of the mountain.

And the four animals sat down on top of their mountain and had a picnic.

The Old-Fashioned Bed

ONCE there was a little boy who loved to visit his grandma. She lived in a little house with a little barn behind it. In the house she kept a yellow kitten and a big black dog. In the barn she kept a frisky nanny goat and a spotted pony. The little boy could play with all of them. And when it was time for him to sleep, his grandma let him sleep in her great big old-fashioned bed.

One day the little boy went to his grandma's house. He played with the kitten. He took the dog for a walk. He fed the nanny goat, and he had a ride on the pony.

After that he had supper. Then it was time for him to go to sleep, so his grandma put him in the old-fashioned bed. She pulled up the covers. She sang him a lullaby. She kissed him good night. And then she tiptoed to the door. She closed the door very gently, but the door said, *"Screeeeee!"*

The little boy sat up in bed and said, "Boo-hoo, boo-hoo, boo-hoo!"

"Oh, my goodness me," said the grandma. She went back in and looked at the little boy. "I'll tell you what. Just this once, for a special treat, I'll let you have the kitten in bed with you."

So she got the kitten. The kitten curled up on the bed. The little boy lay down. His grandma pulled up the covers.

She sang him a lullaby. She kissed him good night. Then she tiptoed to the door. She closed the door very gently, but the door said, *"Screeeeee!"*

The little boy sat up in bed and said, "Boo-hoo, boo-hoo, boo-hoo!" And the kitten stood up and said, "Mew, mew, mew, mew, mew!"

"Oh, my goodness me," said the grandma. She went back in and looked at the little boy. "I'll tell you what. Just this once, for a special treat, I'll let you have the dog in bed with you."

So the grandma got the dog. The dog lay at the foot of the bed. The kitten curled up. The little boy lay down, and his grandma pulled up the covers. She sang him a lullaby. She kissed him good night. Then she tiptoed to the door. She closed the door very gently, but the door said, *"Screeeeee!"*

The little boy sat up and said, "Boo-hoo, boo-hoo, boo-hoo!" The kitten stood up and said, "Mew, mew, mew, mew, mew!" The dog stood up and said, "Ruff, ruff, ruff, ruff, ruff!"

"Oh, my goodness me," said the grandma. She went back in and looked at the little boy. "I'll tell you what. Just this once, for a special treat, I'll let you have the nanny goat in bed with you." So she went out to the barn and got the nanny goat. The nanny goat folded up her legs and lay down right beside the dog. The kitten curled up. And the little boy lay down.

Then the grandma pulled up the covers. She sang him a lullaby. She kissed him good night. She tiptoed to the door. She closed the door very gently, but the door said, *"Screeeeee!"*

The little boy sat up and said, "Boo-hoo, boo-hoo, boo-hoo!" The kitten stood up and said, "Mew, mew, mew, mew, mew!" The dog stood up and said, "Ruff, ruff, ruff, ruff, ruff!" And the nanny goat stood up and said, "Maaaaaaaaaa!"

"Oh, my goodness me," said the grandma. She went back in and looked at the little boy. "I'll tell you what. Just this once, for a *very* special treat, I'll let you have the pony in bed with you."

So out she went to the barn and got the pony. The pony trotted into the house, a little surprised, and leaped right up on the bed and lay down. All the animals lay down. So did the little boy.

Then his grandma pulled up the covers. She sang him a lullaby. She kissed him good night. And she tiptoed to the door. She closed it very gently, but the door said, *"Screeeeee!"*

The little boy sat up and said, "Boo-hoo, boo-hoo, boo-hoo!" The kitten said, "Mew, mew, mew, mew, mew!" The dog said, "Ruff, ruff, ruff, ruff, ruff!" The nanny goat said, "Maaaaaaaaaa!" The pony said, "Naaaaaaaaaaaaaaaay!"

They all stood up, and the big old-fashioned bed fell down! It broke to pieces and they all tumbled onto the floor.

The grandma said, "Oh, my goodness me." She picked up the little boy and put him in a chair. She put the kitten in her box in the corner. She put the big dog under the kitchen table. She took the goat and the pony back to the barn.

Then she got her toolbox. She took her hammer and her screwdriver and put that bed back together. When it was all just as fine as it had ever been, she put her tools away.

And there in the bottom of the toolbox she saw just what she needed.

A can of oil!

The grandma took that oilcan and oiled all the hinges of the door. *Squirt-squirt! Squirt-squirt!*

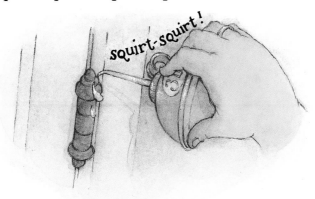

Then she picked up the little boy and put him in the big old-fashioned bed. She pulled up the covers. She sang him a lullaby. She kissed him good night. Then she tiptoed to the door and closed the door very very gently.

The door said, "*Click*."

Then that grandma went into the kitchen and laughed so hard that all her buttons popped off.

CLICK!

The One-Turnip Garden

ONCE there was a family. There was a mother, a father, a big girl, a middle-sized boy, and a very small girl. They had a house to live in, but they had room for only a tiny garden.

"That's all right," said the mother. "We only have one seed, anyway. One turnip seed."

"A one-turnip garden is better than no garden," said the father. "I will dig up the dirt for the one-turnip garden."

"I will plant the seed in the one-turnip garden," said the mother.

"I will water the one-turnip garden," said the big girl. "I will water it every day."

"I will weed the one-turnip garden," said the boy. "I will weed it every day."

"What will I do?" asked the very small girl.

"Oh, you are too little to do anything," they all said. But the very small girl didn't believe it. "I can too do something," she said. But she wouldn't say what it was.

So the father dug the dirt and the mother planted the seed. Every day the big girl watered the one-turnip garden. Every day the boy pulled up the weeds.

And every day the little girl whispered to the turnip. She whispered, "Grow little turnip, grow big. Grow little turnip, grow delicious."

The little turnip grew. It grew big.

"Grow bigger, little turnip," whispered the very small girl. And the turnip grew bigger.

"Grow gigantic, little turnip," whispered the very small girl. And the turnip grew gigantic.

One day the father came home from work and saw that the turnip had grown so big that its green top was taller than the house.

He called his whole family and said, "It's time to pull up our turnip." And he took hold of the turnip and he pulled and pulled. But the big gigantic turnip did not come up.

"I'll help," said the mother. She took hold of the father, who took hold of the turnip, and they pulled and pulled and pulled. But the big gigantic turnip did not come up.

"I'll help," said the big girl. She took hold of her mother, who took hold of the father, who took hold of the turnip, and they pulled and pulled and pulled. But the big gigantic turnip did not come up.

"I'll help," said the boy. He took hold of his big sister, who took hold of her mother, who took hold of the father, who took hold of the turnip, and they pulled and pulled and pulled. But the big gigantic turnip did not come up.

"I'll help," said the very small girl.

"Oh, you can't help," they all said. "You're too little."

"Yes, I can help," said the very small girl. She went over and whispered to the turnip, "Little turnip, you have grown big. You have grown gigantic. Now it is time to come up. Come up, little turnip, come up."

Then she took hold of her brother, who took hold of his big sister, who took hold of her mother, who took hold of the father, who took hold of the turnip.

They pulled and they pulled and they pulled. And the big gigantic turnip . . . *came up*!

And when they ate it, it *was* delicious. At least, that's what *they* said.

The Little Mouse and
Her Grandmother

ONCE there was a little brown mouse who lived in a cozy mousehole with her grandmother.

Every day the grandmother mouse would say, "Good-bye, little mouse. I'm off into the great world to look for food. Perhaps I'll bring you rice, perhaps I'll bring you bean cake, perhaps I'll bring you sweet bun. But if times are hard, at least I'll bring you a bit of candle to chew." And off she scampered.

Every day the little mouse hoped for rice or bean cake or sweet bun. She did not like to chew on a bit of candle.

One day the grandmother mouse was gone a long, long time. The little mouse got very hungry and very tired of waiting. So she poked her whiskers out of the mousehole to see if her grandmother was coming.

She looked one way and called, "Grandma! Grandma!" She looked the other way and called, "Grandma! Grandma!" But she couldn't see her grandmother coming at all.

Then the little mouse noticed something. It was white and very tall. It was the biggest candle she had ever seen.

The little mouse thought, If I climbed to the top of that candle, maybe I could see my grandma coming. And before she thought any more, she ran out of that mousehole and straight up the candle to the very top.

There she sat. She was up so high that she was afraid to move. And she was even hungrier from running so fast.

Maybe this tall candle will taste better than other candles, she thought, and she took a big bite. But it tasted just like any candle.

The little mouse looked this way and that. She couldn't see her grandmother anywhere.

I'd better go home, she thought. Then she looked down the candle. It seemed very very far to the bottom. "It's too far to jump," said the little mouse to herself. "And if I run down I will surely slip. Oh, where is my grandma?"

The little mouse turned one way and called in her loudest voice, "Grandma! Grandma!" She turned the other way and called again, "Grandma! Grandma!" But her grandmother was nowhere to be seen.

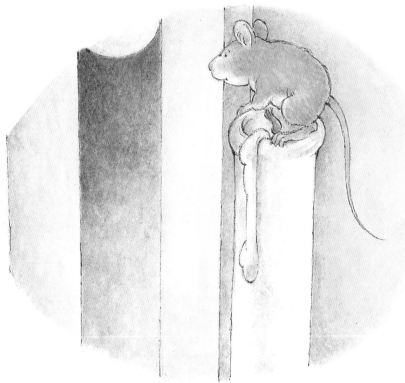

The little mouse looked down at her dear, safe mousehole. Then she had an idea. She curled herself up into a round furry ball and rolled down the candle straight into the mousehole.

She was so nicely curled up that she went right to sleep. She didn't wake up until her grandmother came home with an extra-big piece of sweet bun for her.

"It was so heavy, little mouse, that it took me a long time to get home," she said. "I hope you didn't miss me."

"I missed you," said the little mouse, "but while I waited I learned two things. If I can't run or jump I can roll. And home is the very best place for me."

And she kissed her grandmother and sat down to nibble up all of her sweet bun.

Little Monkey
and the Bananas

LITTLE Monkey lived deep in the jungle. He liked to run up and down trees and swing from branch to branch, but most of all Little Monkey liked to make mischief. And he loved to eat bananas.

On the edge of the jungle there was a village. One day Little Monkey sat in a tall tree and looked down at the houses and gardens of the village.

He thought, Now that would be a good new place to make mischief. I could dance on the grass roofs of the houses. I could turn over the stewpots, and I could eat the bananas growing in the gardens.

Most of the people in the village did not notice Little Monkey high in the tree. But one girl, a girl with bright black eyes, saw Little Monkey, and she said, "Little Monkey, don't ever ever come into the village or you will end up in somebody's stewpot."

So Little Monkey knew he should never go into the village. But still he wanted to.

Then Little Monkey made a plan. One day he went to visit Old Porcupine, the wisest animal in the jungle.

"Grandfather Porcupine," said Little Monkey, "I know you can make magic. Make me a magic charm so that the people will not catch me when I go into their village."

"I can do that, Little Monkey," said Old Porcupine, "but first you must sweep all the dry sticks out of my den, and then you must do exactly as I say or the charm will not work."

"I will do exactly as you say," promised Little Monkey, and he got busy sweeping the dry sticks out of Old Porcupine's den.

Old Porcupine took some bark and some roots and some magic words and he made a charm for Little Monkey. He wrapped it up in a leaf and tied it around Little Monkey's neck. "Now the people will not be able to catch you," he said, "as long as you remember one thing. When you go to the village, don't eat bananas."

"No bananas?" said Little Monkey.

"No bananas," said Old Porcupine. "If you eat those bananas, someone will catch you. Of course, if you stay in the jungle you can eat all the bananas you want."

But Little Monkey said, "I will go into the village. I will dance on the roofs and turn over the stewpots. I will *not* eat bananas." And off he ran.

The first thing Little Monkey saw when he got to the village was the garden of the girl with the bright black eyes. And in the middle of that garden was a tree with a beautiful big bunch of bananas growing right at the top.

Little Monkey stopped and looked up at that bunch of bananas. He wondered if they were ripe. They looked smooth and yellow, but they were so far away. If only he could smell them, then he would know for sure. But he didn't want to do the wrong thing. So he turned around and ran back to Old Porcupine.

"I found a big bunch of bananas," he said. "I *know* I mustn't eat them but can I just climb up the tree and smell them to see if they are ripe?"

"Little Monkey," said Old Porcupine, "you do what you want to do. Just remember *don't eat bananas.*"

Little Monkey ran as fast as he could. He climbed up the banana tree and he smelled those bananas, each and every one. They smelled sweet and ripe. Still, Little Monkey knew that they might look ripe and smell ripe but if he pinched them they might not feel ripe. But he didn't want to do the wrong thing. He slid down the tree and raced to Old Porcupine.

Old Porcupine did not look very glad to see him, but Little Monkey didn't notice. "May I feel the bananas? I'm still not sure they are ripe."

"Do what you want to do. Just remember *don't eat bananas.*"

Little Monkey raced back to the tree and up to the top. He carefully felt each banana from top to bottom. They all felt perfectly ripe, not too hard, not too soft. But Little Monkey shook his head. A banana could look ripe, smell ripe, feel ripe, but when you wrapped your tongue around it you could still get a puckery feeling. He wanted to be sure, but

he didn't want to do the wrong thing. So down the tree he went and along the path to Old Porcupine's den.

Old Porcupine was nowhere to be seen. Little Monkey leaned down and shouted into the den, "Please, Old Porcupine. I promise promise promise I won't eat the bananas. But can I just wrap my tongue around them. Then I will know for sure that they are ripe. Please!"

For a long time he heard nothing. Then from deep in the den came Old Porcupine's voice, "I told you and I told you. Do what you want to do. Just remember *don't eat bananas.*"

Little Monkey nearly flew back to the banana tree and up to the top. He carefully peeled one banana and wrapped his tongue around it. It did not pucker his tongue at all. It felt so velvety and smelled so sweet that Little Monkey closed his teeth and a delicious ripe piece of banana slid down his throat into his tummy. And so it was with all the bananas. And then Little Monkey was so full that he fell asleep right at the top of the banana tree.

The girl with the bright black eyes found him there when she came to tend her garden.

"Oh, Little Monkey," she said. "Do you *want* to end up in a stewpot?" And she shook the banana tree.

Little Monkey opened his eyes. He looked down and saw the girl looking up at him. Then he remembered what Old Porcupine had said.

"Don't eat bananas!" whispered Little Monkey, and he jumped down from the banana tree, clear over the head of the girl. As he ran away into the jungle, he could hear her laughing.

So Little Monkey never did dance on the roofs of the village. No. He stayed in the jungle and ate bananas. As many as he wanted.

The Little Boy Who Turned Himself into a Peanut

THERE was once a little boy who lived with his father on a farm in the middle of a forest.

One day the little boy's father said, "After I finish reading the newspaper, let's go fishing."

The little boy went outside to wait, but his father kept reading the paper and reading the paper.

The little boy waited and waited. Finally he said to himself, "I'll fool him. I'll hide." He looked around for a good hiding place and he saw a peanut lying on the edge of the porch.

"Perfect!" said the little boy, and he turned himself into one kernel of that peanut. And there he was, inside the peanut shell.

Now it just happened that a chicken was walking around the yard and she saw the peanut. Peck! Gulp! She swallowed it.

So where was the little boy? He was inside the peanut shell, inside the chicken.

The chicken went walking over by the trees of the forest, and a hungry fox saw her. Out he jumped. Snap! Gulp! He swallowed the chicken. Then he went trotting through the trees feeling very full.

Now where was the little boy? He was inside the peanut, inside the chicken, inside the fox.

A wolf was prowling through the forest and he saw the fox trotting along. Snap! Gulp! The wolf swallowed the fox.

Now where was the little boy? He was inside the peanut, inside the chicken, inside the fox, inside the wolf.

The wolf felt very full and very thirsty so he ran down to the river and began to drink. Just then, down the river swam an absolutely gigantic fish. The fish opened up its enormous mouth. Snap! Gulp! The fish swallowed the wolf.

And now where was the little boy? He was inside the peanut, inside the chicken, inside the fox, inside the wolf, inside the fish.

The little boy's father finally finished reading the paper. He was ready to go fishing, so he came outside to find the little boy. He looked everywhere. But, of course, he couldn't find him.

"He must have gone off to play," said the father. "I guess I'll go and fish by myself."

When the father got down to the river, the first thing he caught with his fishing pole was an enormous fish. The father looked at that fish and said, "You look very fat. What have you been eating?" And he opened up that fish's mouth and looked down inside, and what did he see? The wolf!

So he pulled the wolf out and the fish swam away.

"Now, Wolf," said the father, "you are looking very fat, too. What have you been eating?" And he opened that wolf's mouth and looked down inside, and what did he see? The fox!

He pulled the fox out and the wolf prowled away.

"Now, Fox," said the father, "you are looking very fat. What have you been eating?" And he opened that fox's mouth and looked down inside, and what did he see? The chicken!

He pulled the chicken out and the fox trotted away.

The father looked at the chicken and the chicken didn't look very fat. But the father said, "Chicken, everybody else has been mighty greedy today. What about you?"

Suddenly the chicken sneezed. *"Ah'choo!"* And out of her mouth popped the peanut.

As soon as the peanut hit the ground out jumped the little boy.

He was so glad not to be inside a peanut

        inside a chicken

        inside a fox

        inside a wolf

        inside a fish

that he *never* turned himself into a peanut again.

The Journey of Tiny Mouse

A TINY little mouse once lived in a hole in a river-bank. All winter long he stayed in his hole, safe from the frost and snow. When spring came he decided to take a journey down the river.

He made himself a boat out of a walnut shell, and for a paddle he used his little garden spade. He climbed into his boat and off he floated. As he floated he sang:

"My boat is a walnut shell, wa-wa-wa!
My paddle's a garden spade, way-way-way!"

He passed a village, and the children called to him from the shore, "Hey there, Tiny Mouse, come and have something good to eat."

"And what is that?"

"A dish of fish."

"No, thank you. I don't want it." And he paddled on singing:

"My boat is a walnut shell, wa-wa-wa!
My paddle's a garden spade, way-way-way!"

He passed another village, and the children called to him from the shore, "Hey there, Tiny Mouse, come and have something good to eat."

"And what is that?"

"Some soup to scoop."

"No, thank you. I don't want it." And he paddled on singing:

"My boat is a walnut shell, wa-wa-wa!
My paddle's a garden spade, way-way-way!"

After a long time, or a short time, he passed another village, and the children called out to him, "Hey there, Tiny Mouse, come and eat something nice."

"And what is that?"

"Sweet cakes on a plate."

"Oh, yes, that's what I want," said the mouse, and he paddled to shore and tied up his boat.

The children placed a plate of nice little cakes before him and he began to eat. They were very small cakes, but he ate so many that his belly grew tight and round.

"Look out!" said the children. "If you eat one more cake your belly will burst."

But Tiny Mouse could not stop. He ate one more cake—and his belly burst.

"Never mind," said the children. "We'll mend you." And they sewed him up again and set him on his feet. Tiny Mouse crept to his boat and away he paddled, very slowly. He couldn't sing because he had forgotten his song. But that didn't matter because

The boat knew its song, "Wa-wa-wa!"
And the paddle its song, "Way-way-way!"
"Wa-wa-wa! Way-way-way!"

Tiny Mouse smiled and soon he was singing, too.

The Magic Drum

ONCE, in a village very far away, an old woman lived in a little house all by herself. She was a bony old woman because she worked very hard and she ate very little, but she was happy.

One day she said to herself, "It's time I went to visit my daughter in the next village." So she made a little bundle of things she would need. Then she locked up her house, and away she went.

The path led through the forest where some wild, wild animals lived. She had not gone very far before she met one of them. It was the jackal, and the jackal is a very crafty person.

"Good morning, old woman," said the jackal. "You are looking very tasty this morning and I am very hungry. I think I will eat you!"

Now the jackal is a very crafty person, but the old woman was even craftier.

"Oh, no, Mr. Jackal, don't eat me now. Look how bony I am. I'm on my way to visit my daughter, and there I will eat and be lazy. Think how fat I will be on my way home. That's when you should eat me."

The jackal thought about eating a fat old woman, and he nodded his head. The old woman hurried on. It wasn't long before she met the wolf.

"Old woman," said the wolf, "I am very hungry and I am going to eat you."

"Oh, no, Mr. Wolf," said the old woman. "See how bony I am. Wait till I come home from visiting my daughter. Then I will be fat and juicy."

The wolf nodded his head, and the old woman hurried on. It was not long before she met the panther.

"Old woman," said the panther, "I am very hungry and I'm going to eat you."

"Oh, no, Mr. Panther," said the old woman. "See how bony I am. Wait till I come back from visiting my daughter. Then I will be fat and juicy."

The panther nodded his head, and the old woman hurried on to her daughter's house. There she forgot all about wild animals. She ate and was lazy and had a wonderful time.

After many days she said to her daughter, "I must go back to my own little house. But, look at me! I am so round and fat that all the wild animals of the forest will want to eat me as I walk home."

Now, the old woman's daughter was even craftier than her mother. She thought of a very good plan. She made a magic drum so big that the old woman could curl up inside it. To make it roll along the old woman had to say:

"Pum, pum, pum
Here I come
In my drum."

"The animals won't even know you are inside the drum," said the daughter. She kissed her mother good-bye and shut her up inside the drum.

The old woman said:

"Pum, pum, pum
Here I come
In my drum."

And the drum began to roll along briskly.

The panther heard the rumbling sound the drum made and said, "That sounds like thunder. How very odd when the sky is blue."

The wolf heard it and said, "That sounds like many horses galloping. It might be hunters. I had better run away."

But the jackal, who is a very crafty person, peered out between the bushes and said, "Why is a drum rolling through the forest? I had better investigate." And he put a rock in the path. The drum hit the rock and stopped. The old woman inside the drum said the magic words:

"Pum, pum, pum
Here I come
In my drum."

"I know that voice," said the jackal. "Old woman, I have caught you now." And he opened the drum and looked at the old woman with very hungry eyes.

The old woman was frightened, but she was still crafty and she said, "Oh, Jackal, before you eat me just let me have a cool drink of water from the river."

"All right," said the jackal, "but I'm coming right with you so you won't run away."

The old woman went down to the river and began to drink. She drank and drank. She drank till she was full of water, right up to her throat.

Then she turned around and said, *"Whoosh!"* and blew all the water straight in the jackal's face. And while the jackal sputtered and rubbed his eyes, the old woman ran away so fast that he could never catch up. She ran straight to her little house and went in and shut the door.

She made herself some tea, and as she drank it she sang:

"Pum, pum, pum,
Here I come
In my drum."

NOTES

Classic nursery tales seem simple, but they have an inherent drama and structure that together involve the young listener in a most satisfying way. For this collection I wanted less-familiar stories that had those invaluable qualities. I have found inspiration in collections of folk tales, in traditional rhymes, and in stories I have heard from storytellers. I have shaped the stories by telling them to many groups of children, giving special attention to the elements of the story that encourage listeners to participate with their voices or their bodies.

It is the nature of stories to travel, and these may have traveled far before they reached the sources where I first encountered them.

FOUR LEGS, FOUR ARMS, ONE HEAD
A retelling of a story from Malaysia, found in *Fables and Folk-Tales from an Eastern Forest*, by Walter Skeat (Cambridge, 1901).

THE FOX AND THE WALKING STICK
Based on a widespread Russian and Ukrainian tale.

THE GREAT BIG ENORMOUS ROCK
Based on an Indonesian children's rhyme:

> The tortoise went up the hill, creepy, creepy, creepy.
> The snake went up the hill, slither, slither, slither.
> The rabbit went up the hill, boing, boing, boing.
> The elephant went up the hill, thump, thump, thump.
> And the big rock went down the hill,
> Bumpity, bumpity, bumpity, *crash*!

THE OLD-FASHIONED BED
Based on a number of similar stories I have heard from several Toronto-area storytellers. At least one version is told in Puerto Rico. I have combined the basic story with a refrain from the following finger play:

> Here is the little boy
> Here is his bed
> Here is his pillow
> Here is his head
> These are his covers

> Pull them up tight
> Sing him a lullaby
> And kiss him good night.

THE ONE-TURNIP GARDEN
Based on a well-known Russian tale.

THE LITTLE MOUSE AND HER GRANDMOTHER
Based on a Chinese traditional rhyme. My version of the verse:

> Up up the candlestick
> Went little Mousie Brown
> She ate a bite of candle
> Then she couldn't get back down
> She called out, "Grandma, Grandma,"
> But Grandma was in town
> So she made herself into a ball
> And rolled herself down.

LITTLE MONKEY AND THE BANANAS
A retelling of a story from central Africa, found in *Wemby, the Singer of Stories*, by Alice D. Cobble (St. Louis: Bethany, 1959).

THE LITTLE BOY WHO TURNED HIMSELF INTO A PEANUT
A retelling of a short version of this story, found in *A World of Nonsense*, by Carl Withers (New York: Holt, 1968), in which he cites as a source *Congo Life and Jungle Stories* by J. H. Weeks (London, n.d.).

THE JOURNEY OF TINY MOUSE
A retelling of a Khanti fairy tale, found in *Northern Lights, Fairy Tales of the Peoples of the North*, compiled by E. Pomerantseva; retold by Irina Zhelznova (English translation, Progress Publishers: Moscow, 1976).

THE MAGIC DRUM
Based on a version of a story from India, found in *Told by the Ayah*, by Advena Hearle (London, 1912).